TROUBLE NEXT DOOR

•• THE CARVER CHRONICLES ••

— BOOK FOUR —

TROUBLE NEXT DOOR

BY Karen English

ILLUSTRATED BY
Laura Freeman

Clarion Books
Houghton Mifflin Harcourt · Boston · New York

Clarion Books
3 Park Avenue
New York, New York 10016

Clarion Books is an imprint of Houghton Mifflin Harcourt
Publishing Company.

www.hmhco.com

The text was set in Napoleone Slab.
The illustrations were executed digitally.

Library of Congress Cataloging-in-Publication Data
Names: English, Karen, author. | Freeman, Laura, illustrator. Title: Trouble
next door / by Karen English ; illustrated by Laura Freeman.Description:
Boston ; New York : Clarion Books, Houghton Mifflin Harcourt, [2016] |
Series: The Carver chronicles ; book 4 | Summary: "Third grader Calvin is
dealing with his next door neighbors moving away — and the school
bully moving in. Meanwhile, competition at the school science fair is
heating up, and Calvin must decide what to do when his data
doesn't prove his theory" — Provided by publisher.
Identifiers: LCCN 2016001080 | ISBN 9780544801271 (hardback)
Subjects: | CYAC: Neighbors — Fiction. | Bullying — Fiction. |
Science projects — Fiction. | Schools — Fiction. | African Americans —
Fiction. | BISAC: JUVENILE FICTION / People & Places / United States / African
American. | JUVENILE FICTION / Social Issues / Bullying. | JUVENILE FICTION /
Humorous Stories. | JUVENILE FICTION / Family / Orphans & Foster Homes. |
JUVENILE FICTION / Boys & Men.
Classification: LCC PZ7.E7232 TR 2016 | DDC [Fic] — dc23
LC record available at https://lccn.loc.gov/2016001080

Manufactured in the United States of America
DOC 10 9 8 7 6 5 4 3 2 1
4500625642

For Gavin, Jacob, and Issac
— K.E.
For Jimmy, Griffin, and Milo
— L.F.

•Contents•

One
Goodbye, the Hendersons

Calvin is pacing the floor in his room. He has a problem. He has to come up with an idea for the science fair. His topic and hypothesis are due on Wednesday, and he can't think of anything. He made the mistake of putting it off even though Ms. Shelby-Ortiz gave the stragglers an extra week. It turns out that Calvin and *all* his friends — Carlos, Richard, and Gavin (yes, even Gavin) — are in the group of stragglers.

As he paces, he runs stupid ideas through his head: how to make a rain cloud in a bottle (Rosario did that in second grade), how to keep a balloon from popping (Gavin did that one last year, and it seemed kind of like a baby project), how to keep an egg from breaking

(That was Richard's project, and, unfortunately, he managed to break eggs during his demonstration. So that project is out of the running. Could Calvin actually do Richard's old project when it didn't work?).

Maybe if he plays just one video game — just to relax and free his mind — an idea will pop into his head like magic. He pulls the controller out from under his bed, turns on the TV, sets it up, and starts a quick game of Wuju Legend.

While he's playing, he listens for his father's footsteps on the stairs. If he catches Calvin, then he'll think that Calvin's mother was probably right about not wanting Calvin to have a TV in his room.

It had been a close call. His mother had argued, "No. Absolutely not."

But his father had said that they could give it a trial run, and if it became

apparent that Calvin couldn't handle it, the TV would be removed. Since then, Calvin has made sure he looks like the kind of kid who can handle having a television in his room. He tries to keep it mostly off — except when he needs to play a video game to relax.

○ ○ ○

Yes, he feels better and ready to go, ready to get started. He claps his hands together and thinks. Nothing. He claps his hands together again, and this time he means it. Still, there are no ideas popping into his head. *I know,* he thinks. *I need a change of scenery. Let me go out to the front porch and breathe in some fresh air. Maybe that'll help my brain.*

Calvin takes the stairs two at a time, marveling at his own athletic prowess. Then he's out the front door, sitting on the top step of the porch, and noticing an interesting hustle and bustle next door. Movers are carrying things to a huge moving van. What? The Hendersons are moving?

The movers are carrying furniture and lamps, and neatly sealed boxes labeled DISHES, BOOKS, LINENS. How could the Hendersons be moving? They've been there forever.

They're an older couple — older than his parents, even. They happen to have three grandsons, all around Calvin's age. Every year since Calvin was old enough to remember, the grandsons have come up from Florida to visit. For the whole summer. It's been like suddenly having brothers and not being an only child anymore. How can the Hendersons be moving? How can they be doing this to him?

His father probably knew all about it. Why hasn't he said anything? Calvin pulls himself up and heads for the kitchen, where his dad is sitting at the table reading the newspaper.

"Dad!"

His father is just raising a coffee cup to his lips as Calvin bursts into the kitchen.

"Hmm?"

"The Hendersons are moving?"

"Oh, yeah." He doesn't even look up from his paper. "I meant to tell you. They're moving down to Florida to be closer to their grandkids."

"That's not fair!" Calvin cries.

"Huh?"

"That's not fair! That means I'm not going to see Robbie, Todd, and Evan anymore."

"Oh," his dad says. "I hadn't thought of that."

Calvin looks at him as if he's grown horns. How could he *not* have thought of that? How could he have kept all this from him? It's major! Doesn't his father care about how he *feels?* Now he puts down his coffee cup and looks as if he's trying to come up with something that will make Calvin feel better.

"Well, you can always write them a letter."

"No, I can't."

"Why not?"

"Because no one writes letters, Dad. They'd think I was crazy if I wrote them a letter."

"Then how are kids pen pals?"

"What's a pen pal?"

"Well, you can call them."

"That's not the same as them being here, right next door."

"Well, I don't know what to say, then."

They just look at each other for a few seconds. Then Calvin flops down in a chair and stares at the box of cereal in the middle of the kitchen table. He feels abandoned all over again. His mom has been gone for a month helping Grandma Kate. She fell and broke her hip, and his mother had to go off to New Mexico to take care of her. She's going to be gone for another whole month.

If his mother were here, they'd be having pancakes right now. He'd be pouring blueberry syrup over a stack of buttermilk pancakes instead of staring at the back of a box of whole-grain cereal.

"Well," his father says, "maybe the new family will have kids. *They* could have three boys." He shrugs. "It's possible." Calvin doesn't respond. After a while his dad says, "They could have five."

Calvin pours himself some cereal in silence. Of course they're not going to have five boys. Does his father think he's some kind of baby who will believe anything?

⦿ ⦿ ⦿

On Sunday, while Calvin is back to thinking and thinking about the science fair — and playing just one more video game — he hears the sound of a truck backfiring next door. He ignores it. Earlier that morning, he'd been busy looking at the calendar on his door and coming up with a plan. A weak plan, but still — a plan. Every day until he comes up with a project idea, he'll spend thirty minutes brainstorming. He'll brainstorm and brainstorm until there's a payoff. More noise next door distracts him then.

It sounds like someone's moving in already. Maybe it will be a family with a kid after all. A boy just his age — one who loves basketball like Calvin does and has the latest Wuju Legend video game. The one Calvin asked for and his father said, "I'm not spending that kind of money on another video game. You'll have to save up for it." And maybe this boy, who'll be living right next door, might loan Calvin his video game whenever Calvin asks.

It's a nice daydream until it's interrupted by a woman's voice — a mean-sounding voice fussing at someone. Calvin hurries to the window and looks down. The slant of the Hendersons' roof hides the woman from view. Still, he can hear her warning someone about "scratching my good table."

Calvin needs to see who this person is and what's going on. He slips downstairs to the living room and looks out the window over the bookshelf. It's a woman with her hair in pink sponge rollers and wearing some kind of housedress that doesn't even look like it's for going outside. Plus, she's got a cigarette in her mouth. Calvin's eyes grow big. Cigarettes are bad for you. Why is she doing something that everybody knows is bad for you?

Suddenly she's looking over her shoulder and calling, "Harper! I need you out here now!"

Harper. Funny — whoever Harper is, he's got the same name as this big boy at school. This big bully, Harper Hall. Calvin and his friends have recently come up with a name for Harper the bully: "Monster Boy," because he acts like a monster, and everybody knows to give him plenty of space when they find themselves near him.

There's no telling what he'll do. He might snatch

your chips from your sack lunch just as you're pulling them out — just as your mouth is watering at the thought of the first crunchy bite. He might belch in your ear as he's passing by, or snatch your ball just as you're getting ready to make a basket. And it doesn't matter if you tell the teacher on recess duty. She'll just fuss at him, and Monster Boy will apologize, but you know he'll *remember*. He'll remember who told on him.

Funny that there's another Harper in the world, Calvin thinks. Now the lady's calling him again. "Get going, Harper. I'm paying these movers by the hour. Get out here and grab a box!"

"I'm coming," that other Harper replies, and he sounds a bit like the one Calvin knows. What a coincidence. And then Calvin sees him, the boy who's being yelled at. Calvin sees him saunter over to an old truck and grab a box off the truck's bed — a box that contains a jumble of junky-looking stuff: old throw pillows and dusty dishes and a stray sofa cushion. The boy has turned away, and his shoulders are a little slumped, but even though Calvin can only see his

back, he knows that it *is* Harper Hall. Harper Hall—
Monster Boy.

Calvin can't believe it. Is this really happening? He closes his eyes and slowly shakes his head. Maybe he's wrong. But when he opens them, there's Harper Hall, ambling up to the front porch steps next door, loaded down with a box full of junk. This must be a dream —or a nightmare. Harper Hall living next door to him? Calvin can only be glad he's watching from the safety of his living room.

Harper makes one shuffling trip after the other with his mouth poked out like he's missing his favorite cartoon or something. And that older lady—probably his grandmother—just stands on the porch and directs everything with one hand on her hip. Calvin almost . . . yeah, he almost feels sorry for Harper.

He looks toward the sound of a news show coming out of the den. His father always watches those news shows on Sunday mornings. Calvin needs to tell him the bad news. But then he wonders if his father will even remember what he's told him about Harper already. He has a way of looking like he's paying attention to Calvin's complaints when he's not. He decides to try anyway.

"Dad, guess what?" he says from the doorway.

"What?" his father says in a distracted tone.

But then, just as Calvin is about to speak, something catches his attention — something on the back of the Sunday paper's sports section. There's one of those optical-illusion things you see from time to time in the paper or in a magazine: the one where you think you're looking at a vase but then it turns into the profiles of two women's faces. He stands there a moment making the illusion go from vase to profiles and profiles to vase, over and over. A light bulb goes off. An idea just pops into his head out of nowhere, and he yells out, "Yes!"

His father looks over his shoulder at him, frowning. "Dad, I have an idea for the science fair! I'm going to do something with optical illusions!"

"What are you going to do?" his father asks, turning back to the television.

"I don't know yet. But —"

"Do you have a theory?" his father asks.

And it comes to Calvin just like that. "Yeah," he says slowly. "I predict that boys can see an optical illusion faster than girls."

"Oh?" His father sounds like he's trying to keep from laughing.

"Yeah. Boys are faster than girls at everything."

Now his father chuckles to himself. "What's your hypothesis? Boys have faster reflexes?"

"Yeah," Calvin says. "That's my hypothesis exactly." Then he realizes that now would be the time to try to get that video game.

"Dad."

"Hmm?" He's back to focusing on the TV.

"If I get first prize ... can you get me the new Wuju Legend game?"

His father sighs, and Calvin knows this is a sign of giving in. "I suppose," he says.

"All *right!*" Calvin knows his father will never go back on his word.

My project is going to be the best, Calvin thinks. *It's going to be awesome.*

"I'm going to find a bunch of great optical illusions, and I'm going to prove who's faster at seeing them, boys or girls. Even though I already know the answer."

"Oh — uh-huh." His father picks up the remote and changes the channel.

Calvin brushes his palms together with confidence. "I'm going to need poster board, Dad. I need to collect my data at recess this week. I want to make some kind of sign or something, so kids will know what I'm doing." His dad is nodding slowly. Suddenly through the open window, there's that woman's loud, brash voice again.

Calvin goes over and looks out. He sees her on the front porch with her hands on her hips, hurrying Harper along as he carries an overloaded box up the walkway.

Calvin still can't believe it. The biggest bully at

Carver Elementary, moving in right next door. Now Harper is carrying a big box of pots and pans up the front steps, still with a pout on his face. Calvin knows that pout. It's the Harper Hall special pout. The one that means he might just pound someone into the ground.

You don't cross Harper. You don't say a ball was out of bounds when you're playing basketball if Harper is on the other team. You don't make fun of him when he's benched. You don't say no if he asks for one of your three Oreos, even though you wanted all three. Harper is a big boy — big for his age. Way bigger than the other fifth-graders, because he did third grade twice.

Calvin finally has a good idea for the science fair, but now he has a new problem — Harper Hall living right next door. Isn't that always how it goes? After one problem has been solved, isn't there usually another one waiting just around the corner?

He interrupts his father again. "Dad," he says, "there's a problem. A major problem."

But his dad doesn't think it's such a big deal. Instead he says it could be a good thing. And by the way, hadn't Calvin been upset thinking there wouldn't be someone his age next door to play with ever again? Well, here's someone from his school. He should look at this as an opportunity. Who knows what the future holds?

Calvin looks at his father like he is speaking some foreign language he doesn't understand. How could his dad be so wrong? Isn't he a grownup? Shouldn't he *know* things?

"He's a bully, Dad," Calvin says now. "Everybody at Carver is afraid of him."

"A bully." He mutes the television. "What makes him a bully?"

Calvin lists everything he knows with examples (which he exaggerates a bit to make his point).

His father looks thoughtful. "What do you think is going on with him?"

"I don't know. I think he's just mad all the time."

"I wonder what would make a person mad all the time."

"I think it's because he gets benched a lot for messing up in class."

His father considers this. Then he shakes his head slowly. "There has to be a reason for all of that. It sounds like he's troubled."

Calvin shrugs. He doesn't know what his father is getting at, but it seems as if he is sticking up for Harper and not understanding how Calvin feels. He realizes that he's going to get no help, obviously. He'll have to take care of this problem on his own.

For starters, Harper is *never* going to find out that he lives next door to Calvin Vickers. *Never.* Not if Calvin can help it. He'll just have to sneak in and out of his own house — starting today. He looks at his father, who's gone back to his TV news show as if the problem is solved.

Calvin's dad usually drives him to school in the morning and then heads on out to his job at Big Barn Food Warehouse. He's the store manager. Calvin has already decided to climb into the car extra early and then duck down until he sees Monster Boy leave. It's a perfect plan.

And then, after school, he'll go to Gavin's or

Richard's or Carlos's house to . . . He stops to figure it out. Yes. To work on his science project with them.

His father will like that. He'll think Calvin and his friends are being responsible and finally getting the hang of using time wisely. This could go on for a while —a long while. Maybe until he graduates from high school. And then he can go away to college and never have to see Harper Hall again.

But that night Calvin does see Harper Hall. He's just about to turn on his bedroom light to get into his pajamas when he glances out his window and across the driveway at the room directly opposite his. The lamp is on and the blinds are open. In the dark, Calvin moves closer to get a better view of Harper punching his pillow around his room and seemingly having a great time doing it. Toss-punch, toss-punch, toss-punch. He can't hear him, but somehow Calvin knows that Harper is putting his all into each punch. He's probably preparing for his next fight, keeping those arm muscles in tiptop shape.

Calvin pulls his desk chair over to the window and

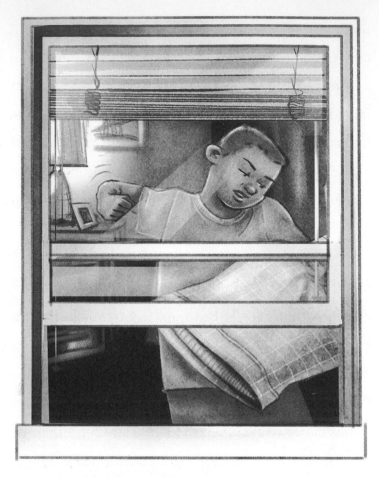

takes a seat. He feels pretty safe sitting in the dark where Harper can't see him.

Monster Boy appears to be having great fun with his pillow boxing. When he tires of that, he sword-fights an imaginary foe with a yardstick. Why is he so angry? Shouldn't he be in bed, anyway?

Two
Monday

Calvin wakes the next morning to sunlight pouring into his room. A new day. He sits up. Then he remembers: Harper. Next door. He looks out the window to the bully's room. Now the blinds are closed. Calvin checks his clock, scrambles out of bed, and hurries to the bathroom to brush his teeth and jump into the shower.

As he gets dressed, he can hear his father in the kitchen talking on the telephone to his mother. He yanks his shirt over his head, dashes to his parents' room, picks up the receiver, and says, "Mom, when are you coming home?"

"Well, good morning, Calvin, and how are you?"

"Fine," he says meekly. "I miss you, Mom. Please come home, but I gotta go." He replaces the receiver and hurries down the stairs and into the kitchen. He grabs the cereal off the top of the refrigerator and a bowl out of the cabinet.

"Whoa," his father says. "Where's the fire?"

Calvin pours the milk and stands at the sink, eating. "I have to get to school a little bit early." It isn't a lie. He feels he really does have to get there early. He finishes his cereal and grabs his backpack from the bottom of the stairs and the car keys off the hall table, then rushes out the door. "Dad, I'll be out in the car," he calls over his shoulder.

Calvin stands a few moments on his front porch, looking toward Harper's house, hoping he won't come out of his front door at the same time. Calvin hurries to the car,

gets the door open, climbs in, and scrunches down in the back seat, his heart pounding in his chest. After a while he shifts his position so he can peek out the window at Harper's front door. All is quiet. Then it opens and Harper comes out. He stands for a moment on the porch and then skips down his front steps, looking not so bad. Not so mean. Then he starts punching the air as he walks all the way down to the corner.

◦ ◦ ◦

"I have something to tell you," Calvin says to Carlos as they put their lunches in their cubbies.

"What?"

"I'll tell everyone at recess." Calvin looks over at the whiteboard and is pleased to see that the class has an open topic for their morning journals. He can't wait to get it all down — how he feels. He settles at his desk, pulls his journal out, and opens to the first clean page.

Bad news, Journal. I mean bad. The worst thing to happen to a guy. Harper Hall has moved in next door to me. And he's kind of *crazy and he's a real scary guy. He's always ready to fight. He loves to fight and walk around being mean. Real mean. Now he's next door and I'm going to make sure he never sees me.*

Calvin doesn't know what else to write. He hopes this isn't one of those times Ms. Shelby-Ortiz will call on someone to read their entry. He's not ready to let the world know about his problem.

He thinks some more. He should write something about that mean grandmother of Harper's. Yeah.

And Journal, he's got this mean grandmother who fusses at him and all he can do is stick out his lip. He doesn't even back talk her. He just does what she tells him to do.

Calvin reads over what he wrote. He likes it. He looks around the room. A lot of the kids are still writing, or trying to. A few are staring at what they've written. He glances across his table at Richard's journal. He's barely written a paragraph, and now he's drawing a picture to go with it. Ms. Shelby-Ortiz lets them do that sometimes. But the drawing should be at the bottom of a page that's almost filled with writing. Richard's drawing of a fancy racing car takes up half the page.

● ● ●

"So what's the news?" Carlos asks as he, Richard, Calvin, and Gavin make their way to the handball courts. That's their recess area for the week. Two girls from their class are already there playing. Calvin frowns. *How did they get ahead of the boys?* he wonders.

"It's bad," Calvin says.

"Just tell us," Richard urges. "Come on."

Calvin decides to draw it out just for fun. "The Hendersons moved."

"Who are the Hendersons?" Richard asks.

"What's wrong with you? They've been my neighbors all my life."

"Oh, yeah," Richard says. "The grandparents of those kids who live in Florida, right? What's so bad about that?"

"Well, it means I'm never going to see Robbie, Todd, and Evan again. But there's something worse," Calvin says.

"Just tell us!" Gavin exclaims. They reach the handball courts and get in line behind Ayanna and Deja and a bunch of other girls. Gavin looks over at the other court, where more kids stand in line.

"Harper Hall now lives next door to me," Calvin says.

Everyone's mouth drops open.

"You're lying," Richard says.

"I'm not lying."

"Oh, dude," Carlos manages after he recovers. "That can't be true."

"It's true."

"No way," Gavin says. "You're joking, right?"

"I'm not joking."

"What are you going to do?" Richard asks.

"I don't know."

"Remember that time he spray-painted some bad words on the back of the auditorium?" Carlos asks. "The janitor had to paint over it."

Calvin nods miserably.

"I heard he beat up this seventh-grader at the movies because the guy looked at him funny," Gavin adds.

Calvin feels a heaviness in the pit of his stomach.

"Oh. And last week I heard he turned over his desk in his classroom because he thought someone was laughing at him," Richard says.

"He got detention," Gavin chimes in.

"My dad says Harper's troubled," Calvin offers.

"What does that mean?" Richard asks.

"I don't know. He's got some kind of trouble, I guess," Calvin says, shrugging. The line moves, and they all shuffle forward. "I gotta stay out of his way. I gotta do everything I can to just stay out of his way."

There's only one more person ahead of Calvin; then it's his turn at handball. He's good at handball. He can really slice the ball — low and fast — and get kids out. He dominates the game, actually.

Three
The Petersons Have a Dog?

Gavin is sure it's okay for everyone to come to his house after school to "work on projects." Parents are more likely to say yes to company if they think everybody's going to be doing homework and encouraging one another, but the boys all know what "working on projects" really means.

"I got the latest Wuju Legend game," Gavin says smugly.

"You have it too?" Calvin exclaims. *Everyone's going to get that game before me,* he thinks.

"Yeah. But before we can play it, we gotta work on our science-fair projects first."

Gavin leads the group into his house through the back door. His sister, Danielle, is sitting on the counter, eating an apple and yapping on her cell. She frowns at Gavin and pulls the phone away from her ear.

"Did Mom say you can have company?" she asks. "Hold on, CeeCee," she says into her phone. "My brother just walked in with three of his little knucklehead friends." She slides off the counter and puts down her apple. She folds her arms and stares at Gavin. "Did she?"

"We're gonna work on our science fair projects," Gavin tells her.

"You get permission?" she asks again, adding a neck roll to her question.

"It's okay," Gavin says to his friends while leading the way through the kitchen, past Danielle, and up the stairs to his room.

"I'm checking with Mom," she calls after him.

"I'm hungry," Carlos announces. "Can't we even get a snack?"

"Later," Gavin tells him.

As soon as they walk into his room, Gavin grabs a small Nerf basketball and aims it at the hoop mounted on the closet. Richard catches it before it hits the floor, and they take turns shooting hoops for a while. Suddenly Danielle is standing in the doorway, squinting at them. "This is working on your science fair projects?" she demands.

Gavin gets up and closes the bedroom door in her face.

"I'm really calling Mom now!" she yells from the hallway. "We'll see about you having company."

Gavin turns back to his friends. "Okay, let's come up with our hypotheses and write them down in our notebooks. Then if my mom gets back from work and asks us what we're up to, we'll have something to *show* her."

"I already know what I'm doing," Richard says, flopping on Gavin's bed. "I'm going to do that volcano with the steamy stuff bubbling up out of it."

"That's an observation kind of thing," Carlos says. "Ms. Shelby-Ortiz said we have to have a *hypothesis.*

We have to have a question and then a prediction. No more observations."

"So, I'll think up a question to go with it." He takes out his notebook from his backpack, opens it, and stares at a blank page.

Calvin is even more sure he'll win first place if all his competition is like Richard. He sits down on the floor and takes out his notebook.

"I read about this experiment where you can use a comb to separate salt from pepper," Gavin says. He has an action figure in his hand and is now sitting cross-legged on the floor. "I can probably come up with a hypothesis if I think about it." He puts the figure aside and pulls his notebook out of his backpack.

Carlos mentions a food-coloring experiment that this girl did when he was in second grade. She put blue dye in the water of a bouquet of white carnations, and after three days the carnations turned blue. "That was kind of interesting," he says.

"Maybe I'll do that." He pulls his notebook out of his backpack, climbs on Gavin's bed opposite Richard, and starts writing something. Then he stops. "No. I got something better." Calvin's ears perk up. He hopes Carlos doesn't have something better. He hopes Carlos sticks with the boring flower thing.

But Carlos says, "I'm going to do something with my geckos." He stops as if to think. "Yeah. I'm going to think up an experiment with their food. Like what food they prefer. What food they'll go to more often or fastest."

"I've never seen geckos go fast to anything," Richard informs him.

"It'll be fast for them," Carlos insists. "Let's just write down our hypotheses and be done for now."

Richard finally begins to write. It's quiet for a while.

Soon Richard puts down his pencil. "Finished," he says. "I got dibs on Wuju Legend."

"It's *my* game," Gavin says. Then he relents. "Okay, Richard, I'll play you first." He closes his notebook. "I'm finished."

This is definitely going to be boring, Calvin thinks as Richard scrambles down from the bed and settles beside Gavin on the rug. Maybe he can run home and get his PSP. It would make the boring waiting for his turn easier. But then he remembers that he can't run home. Funny how you can forget something unpleasant and then have it circle around and hit you right in the gut. *Harper.* He can just see himself climbing his front steps, getting ready to go into his house, right when Harper comes walking down the street punching the air. He can just imagine a slick, scary smile sliding over Harper's face when he sees Calvin.

"Booyah!" Gavin shouts as his video-game player jumps the moat that surrounds the castle. "Booyah!"

Calvin gets up and heads for the door. "I have to run home and get something. I'll be back." He's decided to chance it. Anyway, Harper probably has detention or something. Even if he doesn't, he often stays behind on the playground, going from one area to the other as the whim hits him.

The street is clear as Calvin runs to his house and slips around to the back door. His father's car is in the driveway. Good. He taps on the window pane.

"I thought you were going to Gavin's to work on your science project," his dad says, opening the door. He has papers from work in his hand.

Calvin opens his mouth to say something, but nothing comes out. Then: "Oh, yeah, but I forgot something that I need up in my room." It's not really a lie, because at that moment he does need his PSP so he won't die of boredom watching Gavin and Richard have all the fun.

He runs up to his room, grabs the game from under his bed, and turns to hurry back down the staircase. Then he stops. Is that the sound of a ball bouncing? Next door? A basketball bouncing in the driveway under the hoop attached to the wall above the Hendersons' garage door?

It's got to be Harper, shooting hoops in what is now his driveway. For some reason, Calvin creeps down his own staircase. Then he catches himself at it and thinks, *He can't hear you. He's next door!*

Calvin peeks out the living room window over the bookshelf. It's Harper, all right, practicing lay-ups and messing them up over and over. Calvin almost laughs out loud, but then he remembers that he needs to get back to Gavin's. He can't go out the front door; Harper will see him. He'll have to go out the back. He glances at Harper again. This time his lay-up is successful, and he starts to jump around the driveway and pump his fist in the air.

Calvin slips out the kitchen door with his game shoved into his pocket. He looks back at his house, imagining his father stopping him to ask a bunch of questions. Quickly he scrambles over the fence and into the Petersons' backyard.

It's smart thinking, cutting through the Petersons' yard to Gavin's around the corner. Calvin is just about to race across to the tall chainlink gate leading to the Petersons' driveway when he hears a low growl behind him. He freezes in his tracks. He slowly looks over his shoulder. Staring back at him with teeth bared is some kind of pit bull mix. It looks like half pit bull and half Lab.

The dog has brown fur, blotched with white around both eyes, and white fur on its chest. Its lips are curled back, and Calvin can see long, sharp-looking canine teeth. The dog is making a low, growly, gurgly noise that sounds like it's coming from the back of its throat. Calvin doesn't know if he should look at the dog challengingly, right in the eyes, or look down, to give the dog the feeling that it's the boss.

The pit-Lab is barking ferociously. It's not charging yet, but Calvin has the feeling that it will at any second. He doesn't want to turn his back on it. He can't seem to move, even though Mrs. Peterson could come out of her door any moment and ask him what in the world he's doing in her yard.

He walks backward toward the gate leading to the Petersons' driveway and, beyond that, Gavin's street. He moves slowly, one tiny step at a time. The pit-Lab drops its head and fixes its gaze on Calvin. Its growl sounds full of meanness and threat. Calvin continues to back up, inch by inch, with his eyes locked on the eyes of the demon dog.

Suddenly it's charging at him, barking and biting the air. Calvin turns and races for the fence, grabs the chain links above his head, pulls himself up, and gets one leg over the top before he looks back and sees the pit-Lab yank back on its leash. It was leashed the whole time! But it's a long leash that lets it roam the yard.

Calvin throws his other leg over the top of the fence and stops to look down again. The dog is still throwing itself in Calvin's direction. He's glad he's not on the ground anymore. From his perch on the top of the Petersons' fence he feels like teasing the dog with a "Na-na-na-na-naaaa." But he realizes he doesn't have time. Someone's sure to come out of the Petersons' back door soon, wondering what the fuss is all about. He jumps down and hurries to the sidewalk, looks both ways, and dashes across the street to Gavin's house.

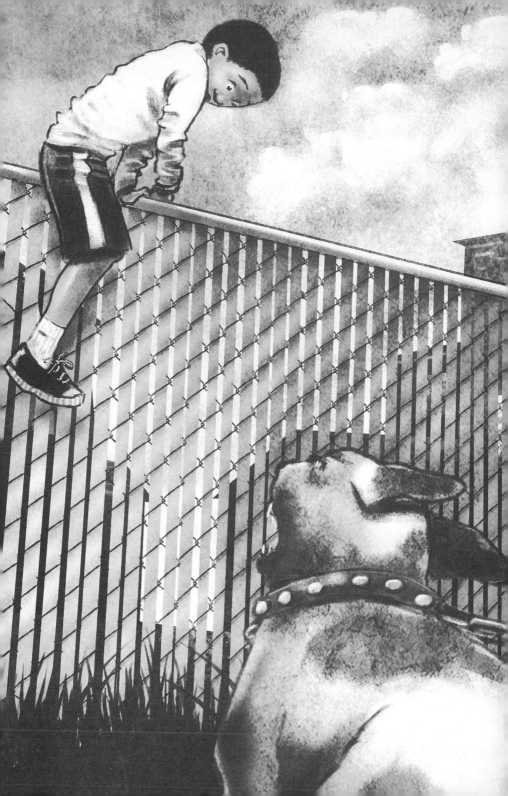

He's got a lot to tell his friends — about Harper, and about the Petersons' new dog.

"How'd you not know they have a dog? What, it never barked before?" Carlos asks like a know-it-all when Calvin tells them what happened.

"I heard the dog, but I just thought the Petersons' neighbors had gotten another dog. They've got two dogs already, so I just never thought about it." Calvin pulls his PSP from his pocket and finds a comfortable spot on the floor. He fires it up.

Four
The Numbers Don't Lie

I'll be in the car," Calvin says to his dad the next morning as he gets up from the table.

"Hold on." His father takes the poster out of his hands, rolls it up, and puts a rubber band around it. "There. Now you can carry it without messing it up."

The night before, Calvin had spent hours working on the materials he'd be using to collect his data. Now he runs through a mental checklist: illusion cards, stopwatch, data-collection worksheet . . . check.

He stuffs everything into his backpack. He's pleased with the poster board he decorated for the table he's going to use. He did a good job. First he wrote in pencil: *Who's Faster — Boys or Girls? (You can find out by taking part in a little experiment.)* Then he went over his lettering with red marker. The red letters against his yellow board look really good.

He thinks of the data-collection sheet that his father helped him make. It has columns and rows, with the columns labeled NAMES, ILLUSION, and TIME. It looks pretty professional. It looks great.

"Thanks, Dad." Calvin takes a bite out of his cinnamon toast as he heads for the door with the poster under his arm.

"Hold up there," his father says.

Calvin stops short with his hand just about to touch the doorknob. He's not surprised. He's been expecting to get quizzed by his dad. He turns and faces him.

"What's the hurry all of a sudden? What's going on?"

"Uh . . . nothing. I'm just anxious to get to school," Calvin says. "'Cause I'm asking Ms. Shelby-Ortiz if I can collect my data today." He turns and eases out the door calmly, pretending he's not in a hurry.

From the car, scrunched down in the back seat, he listens for the sound of Harper's front door opening and closing. When he hears it, he peeks out and sees Harper jump off his porch and head up the street with his backpack slung over one shoulder. Calvin eases back up to a normal sitting position. He wonders what's in the backpack, since Harper is all the time getting benched for not turning in his homework. Just before Harper gets to the corner, he starts punching the air again.

● ● ●

Calvin shows Ms. Shelby-Ortiz his hypothesis. It looks like she's trying to keep from smiling. His father had

the same reaction. Is there something funny about his hypothesis? He can't imagine what. He shows her his poster board and his data-collection form. She seems really pleased.

"I'm impressed," she says. "And, the results should be interesting."

"Can I set up on the playground at recess so I can collect my data? And can Richard or Carlos or Gavin help me?"

Ms. Shelby-Ortiz gives him permission, and he finishes his morning work as fast as possible. Just before recess Carlos helps Calvin carry a small table, two chairs, the poster, the chart, tape, and a stopwatch out to the yard. They finish setting up everything just as the bell rings and students start streaming out of the building.

Calvin takes his place at the card table. Naturally, kids come over and crowd around him, curious about his setup.

"Don't push," Calvin says. "I'm only picking subjects from Room Ten."

He puts five optical-illusion cards on the table, face-down so no one can see them until he's ready. He looks up and begins to point to kids from his class. He chooses Antonia, Leslie, Nikki, Alyssa, and Beverly. They're the girls who Ms. Shelby-Ortiz never has to ask to stop talking or get back to work. Well, Leslie can sometimes be a problem, but she's still better than most, he thinks. They'll probably be really cooperative. Then he chooses Erik, Gerald, Richard, Gavin, and Carlos.

Carlton cries out, "He's choosing his friends! He's choosing his friends!"

"So?" Richard says.

"That doesn't matter," Antonia says.

"Not to you," Carlton protests.

"I can only choose ten total," Calvin explains, "because each kid has to look at five optical illusions, and I have only room for ten on my data sheet."

Carlton frowns. "What's an optical illusion?"

"I can't explain it," Calvin says. "Everybody except Erik, go play! Carlos will come and get you when it's your turn."

He hadn't thought of how he'd handle getting kids to his table. It's a good thing Ms. Shelby-Ortiz allowed him to have a helper.

After the group reluctantly disperses, Erik takes the seat across from him.

For a moment Calvin doesn't know exactly what to do. He should have practiced with his friends, but then maybe that would have been cheating, in a way.

"Okay," he says. He takes one card from the stack and puts it in front of Erik. He keeps it face-down. They both look at the back of the card for a few seconds. Then Calvin fiddles with the stopwatch he borrowed from his father. He doesn't remember what his father told him about how to work it. Erik takes it out of his hand and shows him which buttons to press and when.

Calvin picks up his clipboard with the data sheet attached. He writes Erik's name on the first line. "My name is spelled with a *k*," Erik says.

Calvin erases the *c* and puts a *k*. "All right, when I say go, you're going to turn the card over, and you'll see ten words in different colors spelling out names of colors, but the name is not going to match the color of the word. You have to say the actual color and ignore the word. As fast as you can. Got it?"

"I get it."

"And do it as fast as you can, like I said. See, the left side of your brain's gonna make you want to say the word. It's going to be hard for the right side of your brain to work and say the color. You ready?"

Erik nods, looking confident

Calvin sets the stopwatch and says, "Go!"

Erik turns the card over and just stares at it. "Um," he says while Calvin checks the ticking stop-watch and tries to mentally push him along. "Um . . ." Three long seconds go by, and Erik is still struggling. Finally he finishes and Calvin gets to press stop.

Thirty-five seconds to go through ten color words. Calvin can't believe it.

"I just want to say," Erik protests, "that's not an optical illusion."

"It's one of my tests anyway," Calvin says, and puts a new card on the table face-down. "When I tell you go, turn over the card and tell me the word hidden in the picture."

Erik puts his hand on the card and waits. Calvin pushes the button on the stopwatch and says, "Go."

Erik just stares at the card.

"What do you see?" Calvin asks, to hurry him

along. "It's a word. Come on, what do you see?" Calvin knows he isn't supposed to say anything except the instructions, but this is frustrating. Erik is smart. Why is he acting so dumb?

"Um. I maybe think I see a face," Erik says.

"There is no face," Calvin hisses. "Look for a *word*." Calvin isn't supposed to say that, but he can't help it. The stopwatch ticks on.

"A word?"

"A word, a word," Calvin says, looking at the watch.

"Liar?"

Calvin stops the watch. He sighs. He writes down the time: eighteen seconds.

Next he puts the card with five wolves hidden in the picture face-down and resets the stopwatch. "When I say go, I want you to turn the card over and tell me how many wolves are in the picture. Any questions?"

Erik shakes his head and Calvin frowns. Erik's not very good at this. He should have picked someone else.

Calvin starts the stopwatch and says, "Go!"

Erik says he see one wolf and stays with one wolf as twenty seconds tick away. Then he points out a second wolf. Calvin tries to will him to see three more, but he doesn't. He just stares and stares. "I just see two," he says finally.

Calvin makes a note on the data sheet and puts a two next to it. Then he places the next card face-down in front of Erik. It's a picture with many faces.

"When I say go, look at the picture and tell me what you see — how many objects or people and what they are."

"What they are?"

"Yeah, like men, women, old people." He's giving too much information, he knows. Calvin pushes the button on the stopwatch and says, "Go."

Erik turns the card over and stares at it. "I see an old woman."

"Uh-huh." Calvin keeps his eyes on the stopwatch.

"And an old man."

"Keep going."

Silence. Calvin checks the stopwatch again.

"And a young woman."

Calvin stops the watch. Eleven seconds. Not good. He puts the final picture in front of Erik. It's the one that's a trick question: *How many black dots do you see?* The answer is zero. The white dots only *look* black when your eyes are moving around the page. But if you keep your eyes still, you see only white dots.

Calvin waits for Erik to say zero. He looks at the stopwatch. The seconds are ticking away. *Say zero!* Calvin thinks. *Zero!* But Erik is silent. Finally he looks up. "I think there aren't any black dots," he says. Calvin stops the watch. Fourteen seconds.

Richard doesn't do any better. His times are slower than Erik's, and Carlos's and Gavin's are almost identically slow. Gerald has a hard time following directions. He keeps starting before Calvin even says go, making Calvin wonder, *How are you going to get along in life if you can't even follow the simplest directions?* Gerald is super slow on the color words and only sees one wolf.

Calvin forges ahead. After the boys have had their turns, Calvin sends Carlos off to get Antonia. She comes over and sits in front of him. She looks at him with one eyebrow raised as if to say, *What are you waiting for?*

Calvin explains the procedure, and Antonia looks a little bit bored. They start with the color cards. Antonia goes through them in fourteen seconds and then gives him a look that says, *What else you got?*

Calvin puts the card with the hidden word face-down. With a tiny, confident smirk on her face, Antonia sits back and crosses her arms.

"When I say

go, turn the card over and say the word hidden in the picture."

She sighs. Calvin starts the stopwatch and says, "Go."

Antonia turns over the card and says, "Liar."

"What?" Calvin asks.

"The card says *liar.*"

Calvin writes down the time: three seconds.

She leans back even further, stretches out her legs, and waits for the next card.

The one where you count the wolves in the picture is no challenge for Antonia either. Calvin watches with dismay as she places a finger with pink nail polish on each of the five wolves in seven seconds. "Five," she says, looking up at Calvin. "There are five wolves."

As soon as the three-faces card is turned over, she states that there are three people: an old man, an old woman, and a young woman. For the black-dots card, she announces the answer is zero in three seconds.

Calvin frowns. It's almost as if she's seen all the cards before. Maybe the illusions were in some magazine she reads — *Highlights* or some Brownies magazine. She couldn't be that fast.

Next comes Nikki. She sits down smiling, as if taunting him. She does just okay on the color cards, but sees the word *liar* on the hidden-word card almost immediately after he puts it down. On the wolves card, he barely gets the question out and she says, "Five. There are five wolves on that card."

That cinches it. The girls must have seen that one before. But of course he can't prove it.

Though they don't do as well as Antonia and Nikki, Beverly, Alyssa, and Leslie do better than all the boys. Calvin doesn't understand how this happened. His experiment is a complete failure. The results don't match his prediction even a little bit. What went wrong? It must have been his subjects. He chose the wrong subjects. He needs new ones. He looks around the schoolyard just as the bell rings, signaling the end of recess — and the end of his data collection.

Five
It's Not Nice to Eavesdrop

Calvin is still thinking about the disappointing results the next day when Ms. Shelby-Ortiz passes out blue construction paper and lined white paper to the class. It's for the invitations they're making to formally invite their parents to the science fair.

Deja, who now sits across from Calvin and next to Richard at Table Three, grabs four markers — though she knows she can only use one at a time — and slips them into her desk.

Ms. Shelby-Ortiz doesn't allow them to hoard markers in their desks. All the markers that aren't being used have to remain in the marker can that sits in the middle of the table. And Deja knows that, Calvin thinks.

Plus, Deja hasn't even bothered copying, in neatest handwriting, the paragraph inviting parents to Carver Elementary School's annual science fair, nor has she written down the pertinent details, such as the date, location, and time. Her parents won't even know that the science fair is next Friday after school if she doesn't bother to include that information. She's trying to jump to the fun part — drawing flowers all over and coloring them — before doing the work.

Calvin is about to point out all the things she's doing wrong when Ms. Shelby-Ortiz says, "I don't want to see anyone using markers before I've approved their actual invitation. In other words, if I see anyone decorating their invitation before I've approved it, that person will be starting over."

Calvin looks at Deja pointedly. She rolls her eyes at him but doesn't return the markers. Calvin's hand shoots up. Slowly, with her eyes on Calvin the whole time and her mouth poked out, Deja puts the markers back in the can. Calvin lowers his hand, looks at the board, and sighs. He feels such pressure when he's ordered to write in his best handwriting.

"Oh," Ms. Shelby-Ortiz says, "there's one other

really exciting thing about this year's science fair." She pauses for dramatic effect.

Calvin thinks that sometimes what Ms. Shelby-Ortiz says is exciting is only exciting to her. He waits politely but doesn't expect much.

"This year we're going to have a panel of parents judging your projects. Each parent on the panel will have a scorecard to judge each project and will give points based on hypothesis, interest level, display, results, conclusion, etc. I'll go over it in more detail later."

"But Ms. Shelby-Ortiz," Rosario says without raising her hand and waiting to be recognized, "parents will give their own kids extra points."

Ms. Shelby-Ortiz overlooks this infraction. "That's where Mrs. Marker from the front office comes in handy. She's going to serve as a kind of roaming substitute for the parent who needs to excuse himself or herself because his or her child is being scored."

Rosario squints as if she's mulling over this news. Ms. Shelby-Ortiz goes on. "It's possible that the first-place winner is right here in Room Ten," she says with a big smile on her face. "Fingers crossed."

○ ○ ○

The good thing about doing extra stuff that's not part of the morning routine is that it takes time away from the regular schedule. When the invitations are finished, the class only has time to do a little reading before recess.

"There's Monster Boy," Richard says, pointing at Harper making his way to the benches. "Your *neighbor.*"

"Don't point," Calvin says quickly.

"Why? He doesn't even know he lives next door to you."

Calvin watches Harper take his usual seat on the bench. He puts his elbows on the table behind him and surveys the playground. Calvin wonders about him. Why is he so angry? Why doesn't he care that he gets benched every few days?

"So Harper lives with his grandmother?" Carlos asks.

"I guess she's his grandmother," Calvin answers.

"And she's mean?"

"She sounds mean."

"Maybe that's what makes him mad," Richard says.

"Maybe," Calvin agrees. Then he hurries ahead to be the first in line at the handball court.

○ ○ ○

"Let's go by Delvecchio's and get some snacks," Carlos suggests as the group heads down the street when school lets out. Calvin managed to get permission to go with his friends to Richard's after school for an hour to continue work on his science-fair project. Richard has the new PSP, and Calvin just wants to preview it a little bit so he'll know whether to start bugging his parents for it or not.

It isn't until they're almost at Mr. D.'s store that Calvin remembers he left the invitation to the science fair in his desk at school. Ms. Shelby-Ortiz is giving points for returning it in a timely manner, which means tomorrow.

"Shoot," he says as everyone turns toward Ashby and Mr. D.'s. "I forgot my invitation. It's in my desk."

"So bring it home tomorrow," Richard says.

"Our table needs the points, and I don't want to be the one who gets blamed when we don't have a one hundred percent responsible table." Calvin sighs and turns back toward Carver Elementary.

Through the classroom door's small window, Calvin can see his teacher at her desk. It looks like she's correcting the spelling test they took the previous Friday. He taps on the window, and she looks up and smiles.

"Ms. Shelby-Ortiz," he says, entering the room, "I just have to get my invitation to the science fair out of my desk."

"What's it doing in your desk?"

"I accidentally left it there."

"But I remember telling everyone before our class lined up for dismissal to put their invitations in their backpacks. Didn't you hear me tell the class that?"

Just then he *does* remember, but he doesn't remember why he didn't do it. Should he admit that? Better not. "Uh," he says.

"Look at the time you've wasted having to come all the way back to school when you could be already at home doing your homework."

Calvin thinks: *No, I would not be at home doing homework. I'd be buying candy right now to eat at Richard's while I check out his new video game and just generally mess around.* But he knows he shouldn't tell his teacher that.

He knows he probably wouldn't have gotten to his homework until after dinner, when his father was tired and wanting to just relax and not be hunched over a word problem, taking him through the steps: *Underline what's being asked. Cross out all the extra information that you don't need to solve the problem. Solve the problem using all the relevant information.*

But instead of saying all that, he simply stares at her.

Now she's talking about responsibility and developing good habits because they'll serve him in the future and on and on, and he stops listening. Can he just get the invitation out of his desk and be gone? He stands there politely, waiting it out, until finally she finishes.

When she goes back to her paper correcting, he scoots to his desk and plucks out the invitation, happy that it's easy to find. He can just imagine what it would have been like if he'd had to pull everything out of his desk to search for it. He'd probably get another lecture on the importance of being organized, the time it can save, and blah, blah, blah.

He holds it up so she can see it. "Got it, Ms. Shelby-Ortiz."

She smiles, probably satisfied that she got to engage him in a teachable moment. Ms. Shelby-Ortiz is always talking about teachable moments, whatever those are.

As Calvin leaves the classroom, he's got chips on

his mind. He'll swing by Mr. D.'s on his way to Richard's. He starts whistling as he walks down the hall, imagining the taste. He passes Mr. Willis's room and sees he's right in the middle of a parent-teacher conference . . . with Harper and his grandmother? Calvin backs up out of view and presses himself against the wall so he can listen.

Mr. Willis is listing Harper's latest infractions. He's telling Harper's grandmother about Harper going to the restroom and throwing pieces of wet paper towel onto the restroom ceiling. "Do you know how troublesome it is for the janitor to remove clumps of wet paper towel off the ceiling?"

"I do, I do," Harper's grandmother says. "But I don't know what to do with this boy."

Mr. Willis turns to Harper. "What do you have to say about all of this, Harper?"

Calvin takes a peek around the door frame and sees Harper slouched in his seat with his mouth poked out, picking at a fingernail. "I dunno," he says.

"Is that all you got to say to your teacher?" his grandmother asks. "What's wrong with you?"

Calvin puts his hand over his mouth to stifle a

laugh. That's when he feels a hand on his shoulder. Not a kid hand. A grownup hand, heavy and pressing down a bit like it means business. He looks up to see the frowning face of Mr. Brown, the principal.

"What are you doing?" he asks.

"Nothing," Calvin says, and he knows it's a stupid response even as it's coming out of his mouth.

"Didn't anyone ever teach you not to eavesdrop?"

Calvin can't remember anyone actually *teaching* him not to eavesdrop — because maybe he's never done it before, that he can remember — but he nods his head anyway and looks down. Here's the thing he doesn't want: He doesn't want Mr. Brown to have a bad opinion of him. And it might already be too late for that, because of that stupid newsletter

Deja put out earlier in the year — she and her friend Nikki.

Ayanna had gotten her book-fair money stolen, and in that newsletter, which he hopes Mr. Brown never saw, Deja had kind of pointed the finger at Calvin. She'd sort of mentioned him as a prime suspect, using his initials. Everyone knew CV was meant to be him. And he's never stolen *anything*.

Deja was probably thinking about the time when Ralph traded his Hot Wheels Pharodox for Calvin's Lego key chain. The key chain had impressed Ralph for a little while, and he must have traded the car without thinking and then realized there was nothing much to do with a key chain except put your keys on it — but he had no keys.

So Ralph tried to trade back, but Calvin wasn't having it. Ralph gave the key chain back anyway, and Calvin simply put it in his desk along with the Pharodox. If Ralph wanted to give him back his key chain, that was his choice; Calvin would take that too. But then Ralph went to Ms. Shelby-Ortiz and accused Calvin of stealing the Hot Wheels car, and the whole class had to listen to her lecture about bringing toys to school.

Of course, the Pharodox was in his desk because it was *his*. But then Deja put it in her neighborhood newsletter that he, Calvin, was a thief. *Not fair!* Especially if Mr. Brown read that about him. Calvin was so happy when the newsletter fizzled out and Deja and Nikki had to print retractions of all the things they got wrong.

"I think you need to run along and mind your own business," Mr. Brown is saying. "Don't you think so?"

"Yes, Mr. Brown."

"Good."

Calvin hurries down the hall, deciding to go straight home instead of to Mr. D.'s. He's kind of lost his appetite for chips. Richard and the others will probably wonder what happened to him. He'll explain tomorrow that he just decided to go home.

Six
Dad's Very, Very, Very Lame Idea

The next afternoon, Calvin comes straight home from school. He doesn't have to sneak in or watch his back because Carlos told him that Harper has detention— *again*. Calvin's father is at the sink, washing broccoli. Calvin stands there a while, trying to overcome his gag reflex and thinking, *What other things might go wrong today?*

His dad glances over at him and says, "So how did it go yesterday? It's been so busy at work, I forgot to ask." Now he looks all eager.

Calvin stares at the broccoli. "It was fine," he says, and he knows his face doesn't match his words. "Fine."

"Well, what happened? Did you collect your data?"

"Yeah."

"So what were the results?" Calvin's dad wipes his hands on a dishtowel and turns to look at him.

"The girls were faster than the boys."

His father looks like he wants to laugh. Calvin doesn't understand what that's all about, but he doesn't like it.

"All of them?" Dad asks, still looking like he's about to laugh.

"All of them."

"Well, you have to accept the results."

But Calvin was counting on different results. He counted on showing up the girls. It's going to be hard to be excited about girls being faster than boys. He shakes his head.

"You know," his father tells him, "you just have to accept it. Girls are faster at some things — boys are faster at others."

Maybe that's true. But that doesn't mean Calvin shouldn't be disappointed in the results. Sometimes a parent just can't understand a thing the way a kid can. First of all, Calvin's dad doesn't understand that this means that his science fair experiment didn't work out. It *was* a big deal to sit there and see the girls do way better than the boys. Especially since Calvin even included Erik Castillo, the smartest boy in the class, on his list of subjects. *The smartest boy in the class.* And the girls did better than him. What is wrong with that Erik? Maybe he needs glasses.

Later, in his room, Calvin pulls out his data sheet from his backpack. He stares at it. For just a moment — the tiniest moment — Calvin toys with the idea of slightly, kind of . . . altering the results. Just a little bit. Just so the girls don't show up the boys *so much*. He almost reaches for a pencil on his desk. But then he stops himself. Best to leave everything as is.

Anyway, the fact that he used real human subjects might just give him a leg up over the other kids' projects.

Richard had tried to ruin Calvin's optimism when Calvin happened to mention that fact at recess. "You don't *know* that you're the only one who used real subjects in your project," Richard had said. "A bunch of other people could have too."

Calvin had thought, *But I bet you there* aren't *a*

bunch of people who used real human subjects besides me. He didn't say it, though, because Richard would have come back with reasons why he thought other kids used real subjects, and Calvin didn't want to hear it.

Calvin's dad pokes his head into Calvin's bedroom to remind him to get started writing up the results of his project. "Don't put it off until the last minute. Remember, the science fair is sooner than you think."

He knows the science fair is close, and he knows, as he sits at his desk staring at his data sheet again, that he'll have to record the truth: When it comes to optical illusions, the girls he used as subjects were faster than the boys.

That night, at dinner, Calvin's dad comes up with a "great idea." It seems he was taking the trashcans to the curb in the morning when he saw Harper's grandmother, Mrs. Jeffers, struggling with hers. Apparently he introduced himself and insisted on helping her. Then they got to talking. (This is where Calvin gets a little sinking feeling in the pit of his stomach.) Of course, the subject of Harper and her struggles with his behavior came up.

Calvin takes a bite of his mashed potatoes and waits.

"She was telling me how she wished Harper had a man's influence in his life — someone who could show him a little attention." His father pauses, and Calvin thinks, *Here it comes.*

"So I thought it would be nice if we invited him to go to the movies with us on Saturday to see *The Thing from Another Planet Three.*"

Calvin puts his fork down. This is his father's great idea? He looks at the table and frowns, to show his father how he feels about it.

"I think that kid just needs someone to be nice to him," his father continues.

"But it was only going to be the two of us.

Anyway, Harper probably hasn't even seen *The Thing from Another Planet One* and *Two*. He's not going to even know what's going on. And if I have to explain everything, that's going to ruin the movie for me and—"

His father stops him right there by holding up a palm. "I'll explain everything on our way to the movie. Don't worry. I'll take care of it."

"You don't know him, Dad."

"Maybe we should get to know him."

"He's not someone you can get to know! When's Mom coming home?" Calvin adds. Suddenly *every-thing* is not to his liking.

"You know when she's coming home. In another month or so." His father shakes his head as if he's a little bit disappointed in Calvin. But Calvin's the one who's more disappointed. He's been looking forward to this outing with his father. They have their own moviegoing routine: getting there early enough to see *all* the previews, getting a big tub of popcorn and two giant boxes of Milk Duds to sprinkle in the popcorn and two large cherry slushies, getting seats close to the aisle so they don't have to step over people if one of them has to go to the bathroom. Heaven. Having Harper along is going to ruin all of that. It's not fair.

● ● ●

The next day at the lunch table, Calvin's friends can't believe what Calvin's father is up to. "Why's he doing that to you?"

"He thinks Harper needs people to be nice to him. That if he had more kindness shown to him, he'd behave better," Calvin says.

"Harper's probably going to make it miserable for you," Gavin says, opening up his bag of chips. Richard holds out his hand, and Gavin shakes one chip into his palm.

"Just one?" Richard protests.

"I don't hardly have any. They put a whole bunch of air in the bags."

Gavin turns to Calvin. "Betcha he'll steal something from the concession stand and then *you* will get in trouble," Gavin says.

"No," Carlos says. "The candy and stuff is behind glass."

"Not all of it," Gavin insists. "Better keep your eyes on him."

"Or he could get into a fight with another kid," Richard adds. "Over nothing."

"He's not going to get into any fight," Calvin says, realizing he's actually sticking up for Harper.

"He might," Richard tells him. "Maybe a kid will look at him funny. You never know."

For some reason Calvin doesn't think that Harper is going to pound anyone into the ground at the movies — not while he's with Calvin's dad, at least.

"So now he's going to know you live right next door to him," Carlos observes.

"And that you've been hiding out from him," Richard adds.

"He's not going to think I've been hiding out from

him. He's just going to think we haven't seen each other. Yet."

"Hope he doesn't get jealous that you have a dad and he just lives with his grandmother."

Calvin frowns — because that *is* a possibility. He hadn't even thought of that.

Seven
The Thing from Another Planet 3

The movie starts at two. It's one fifteen and Harper still hasn't shown up. Calvin paces the living room floor, throwing his arms up from time to time. "I can't believe it," he says under his breath. "I knew he'd find a way to ruin things."

His dad is in the kitchen, washing his hands after working in the garden. "He's not here, Dad, and the movie starts at two. We're going to miss the previews."

"The *previews* start at two," his father corrects him. "Why don't you just run next door and see what's delaying him?"

"I don't want to go and see what's delaying him." He's never even spoken to Harper. Never.

"Get going," his father says in a tone that means

there'll be no discussion. Calvin sighs and starts out the door.

When he rings the bell, he has to wait a while before Harper's grandmother opens the door. She has a cigarette in her hand. He stares at it. She laughs and puts it out in an ashtray on the coffee table. There are still boxes stacked in the living room. Someone must've slept on the sofa, because a sheet and blanket are balled up at the end of it.

"I'm here for Harper," Calvin says.

"Harper?" she repeats.

"He's going to the movies with me and my dad."

"Oh, right." She turns her head and calls, "Harper! That boy from next door is here. He and his daddy are supposed to be takin' you to the movies. Now don't keep them waitin.'"

Calvin waits.

"Harper!" she calls again.

Still nothing. She looks at Calvin and says, "You go on up to his room and get him. He's down the hall, first door on the right. Go on now and hurry him along."

Calvin doesn't want to go on up there and hurry Harper along. That's the last thing he wants to do. He looks at the darkened staircase, and feels a sense of dread. He looks back at Harper's grandmother, hoping she'll have another suggestion. But she just looks at him as if waiting for him to follow her instructions.

"Go on now," she says as if she can read his mind.

He swallows. He can feel her watching him as he walks carefully up the stairs. The first door on the right is open. Harper is lying on his bed, staring at his ceiling. He looks over at Calvin but doesn't say anything.

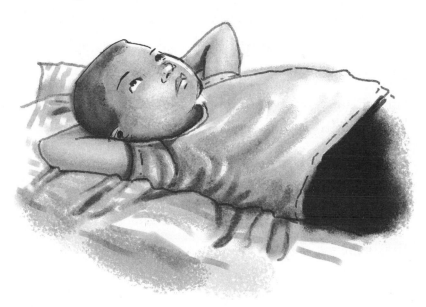

Calvin doesn't think he's ever been this close to Harper before. He doesn't know what to say. Finally he manages, "Uh, my dad's waiting for you."

"You go to my school," he says.

"Uh . . . yeah," Calvin says and braces himself.

"I have to wash my face and brush my teeth." Harper gets up and passes a little too close to Calvin as he crosses in front of him to get to the bathroom down the hall. Calvin frowns. Shouldn't he have already done that?

While he's gone, Calvin looks around. The walls are covered with posters of the most valuable players from different basketball teams. Calvin is a little surprised to see this side of Harper — that he's a person with regular interests like any other boy. There's a framed photograph of a woman about Calvin's mother's age on Harper's dresser. Calvin is looking at it closely when Harper walks back into the room.

Calvin feels as if he was caught being nosy, so he's quick to explain. "I was . . . I was just wondering who this person is," he says.

"That's my mother," Harper says glumly.

"Your mother?"

"Right."

"Where is she?"

"Around."

"You don't live with her?" Calvin asks.

"No."

"My mom's gone," Calvin says — just to have something to say. "Because my grandmother broke her hip and my mother has to take care of her."

Harper doesn't say anything. It's almost as if he didn't even hear. Then he says, "My mom's homeless."

Calvin is caught completely off-guard. He looks at the picture again. Harper's mother doesn't look homeless. She's standing next to a tree, laughing and shielding her eyes. She has on regular clothes and everything.

Calvin doesn't know what to say. Then he asks, "Is that why you live with your grandmother?"

Harper looks puzzled.

"Mrs. Jeffers," Calvin says.

"She's not my grandmother. She's my foster mother."

Foster mother? Now Calvin's doubly surprised. He doesn't think he's ever met a foster kid. He knows about them, but he doesn't remember how. TV, probably. Or maybe he heard his mom and dad say something about foster kids. Don't they have sad, sad lives because their mothers and fathers can't take care of them and they have to go to a foster home? And aren't some of those homes not good? He thinks about Mrs. Jeffers and her cigarettes.

"Let's go," Harper says in a bored tone.

He doesn't even look happy to be going to the movies with Calvin and his dad. It must be hard for Harper to be happy, Calvin thinks.

"Where's your dad?" Calvin asks.

"Somewhere," Harper says, as if there's nothing more to add.

● ● ●

Before they leave, Mrs. Jeffers puts money in Harper's hand — probably for the movie tickets and snacks. They cross the driveway back to Calvin's house in silence, and as soon as they step into the living room, Harper asks if he can use the bathroom.

Calvin's heart drops. He looks at his watch.

"Sure," his dad says. "Down the hall and then to the right." He points the way.

Now it's more waiting. And waiting. Soon Calvin is wondering what's taking Harper so long. Just as Calvin's dad is ready to send Calvin to check on him, he comes lumbering back down the hall. *Finally,* Calvin thinks.

In the car, Calvin's been relegated to the back seat, and he wonders why. His dad probably wants Harper to feel welcome. Calvin guesses he doesn't mind all that much. His dad begins to do his usual routine: asking a lot of questions. "So, Harper, how do you like your new neighborhood?"

"It's okay," he says, with his face aimed out the window.

Now that Calvin has a close-up view, he's looking at Harper very carefully. Harper could use a haircut or maybe just a brush run through his hair. His cotton shirt is a little wrinkled, and he has a sad slump to his shoulders. He doesn't look mad. He looks unhappy. Calvin almost feels sorry for him.

"What about school?" his father asks. "What's your favorite subject?"

Calvin wonders why grownups always ask a kid that question. Maybe Harper doesn't have a favorite subject. Come to think of it, what's his own favorite subject? Calvin wonders. *Science.* It occurs to him, just then, that he likes science.

Harper doesn't answer. Then, out of the blue, he says, "I like working in gardens. I'm going to be a gardener." Calvin can feel his dad's approval.

"Now that's a really original answer. I'm betting you'll make a great gardener," Calvin's father says.

Calvin sees Harper glance quickly at his dad, as if to see if he's serious or not. Then he smiles and looks down like he's suddenly embarrassed.

● ● ●

Calvin notices that Harper doesn't pull out his money to pay for his own movie ticket but instead lets Calvin's dad pay for everything. He buys their popcorn and Milk Duds and cherry slushies, plus Raisinets and another large cherry slushie for Harper. But when Calvin's dad passes the candy and drink to Harper, Calvin is surprised to hear Harper say, "Thank you."

The theater is filling up fast, but they find seats on the aisle halfway up just as the previews begin. Harper goes first, then Calvin's dad, then Calvin. Calvin likes the aisle seat. He doesn't really care about

who sits where, as long as he has the seat next to the aisle. Harper can sit next to his father, because Calvin has his father all the time.

He digs into the popcorn and Milk Duds. Great combination. The previews are just as entertaining as Calvin expects *The Thing from Another Planet 3* will be. He feels excited. He glances at Harper. He's staring at the screen with a blank look on his face. Funny how he's seeming less and less like a monster boy.

Thirty minutes into the movie, he taps Calvin's father on the shoulder. "Can I go to the bathroom?" he asks.

With his eyes still on the screen, Calvin's father

says, "Sure." Calvin is immediately suspicious. Didn't Harper just go to the bathroom at Calvin's house?

Fifteen minutes later, during a really exciting chase scene between a humanoid and a robot, Calvin's father nudges him. "Go see what's taking Harper so long."

"Dad." Calvin doesn't want to leave the theater — especially in the middle of this chase scene.

"He might be sick," his father whispers. "You need to go check."

What Calvin wants to know is why his father can't go check. Why does he have to send him?

He sighs, pulls himself up, and makes his way down the aisle. He takes the steps two at a time, exits the theater, and starts down that long hallway to the big lobby. He can see the bathroom with the sign of a figure of a man over the door. He pushes it open, expecting to see Harper standing in front of a sink drying his hands or in a stall being sick to his stomach.

The bathroom is empty. Empty? So where is Harper? This guy is making Calvin miss the movie! He looks in every stall again, just to be sure. All vacant.

He stomps his foot in frustration. This is his father's fault. Why did he think it was a good idea to invite Harper anyway? Harper, of all people? He tried to tell his father that there would be some kind of problem, some kind of glitch.

Forget it, Calvin thinks. He's just going to go back to the movie that he's been wanting to see for weeks. But as he's crossing the lobby, he sees Harper come out of one theater and go into another. *What is he doing?* Calvin wonders. He looks up to see the marquee announcing the latest feature-length Dooly Duck cartoon. A cartoon? He glances at the three teenagers behind the refreshment counter. They're busy talking to one another. He checks the girl taking tickets. She's checking something on her cell phone.

With his eyes still on her, he slips into the theater. It's half full of little kiddies and their mothers or fathers or babysitters. He scans the rows, searching for Harper. A few of the moviegoers look over at him, but the eyes of the audience generally remain on the screen. At the very back, in the middle, with vacant seats surrounding him, sits Harper.

Calvin climbs the aisle and stands next to the

last row. "Pssst," he whispers, to get Harper's attention. But Harper doesn't hear him, apparently. In fact, Harper bursts into laughter at something on the screen. Calvin looks back to see Dooly Duck break dancing. It's a funny sight. Calvin almost laughs too, but he catches himself. "Pssst," he whispers a little louder, catching the attention of a teenage girl, who's probably someone's older sister or babysitter, a few rows down. She gives him a big disapproving stare.

He ignores her. "Harper!" he whispers, and finally Harper looks his way. Calvin makes a motion for Harper to follow him out of the theater. He can feel his reluctance as he shuffles down the aisle behind Calvin.

"What are you doing?" Calvin says as soon as they are back in the lobby.

"What do you mean?" Harper looks genuinely puzzled.

"Why are you in *that* movie instead of the one with me and my dad?"

"I seen that one already."

"What?" Calvin stares at Harper in amazement.

"Then why didn't you tell us? Why did you agree to go?"

"My foster mother wanted me to. She said I don't have any friends and I need friends. And you live right next door." Harper looks at Calvin as if that's that.

Calvin stands there, staring at Harper. He doesn't know what to make of him. He just doesn't *get* him. "My father sent me to find you."

"Okay," Harper says. Calvin is surprised by how cooperative he is.

He follows Calvin back to their seats in the theater showing *The Thing from Another Planet 3*.

"Are you okay?" Calvin's dad asks, probably thinking Harper was in the bathroom so long because of some kind of ailment. Harper nods his head.

It's too late for Calvin, however. He tries hard to get back into the movie, but he can't. He'll have to see it again. He sneaks a look at Harper and sees that he continues to have a completely blank look on his face.

"I don't get him, Dad," Calvin says later that night over Chinese takeout. "He didn't even act like he had done something wrong or that you might be worried when he didn't come back. I don't think he knew that you just don't do stuff like that."

"Let's not be too hard on him. We don't know what he's going through. Pass the hot mustard, please."

Calvin thinks about this. He thinks about it as he's brushing his teeth before bed. He thinks about it as he turns off the light and stares at Harper's bedroom window with the blinds closed. He wonders what it would be like to be a foster child — to live in a strange person's house, sleep in a strange bed, eat strange cooking.

Mrs. Jeffers is . . . *okay*, he guesses, but she's not Harper's mother. A real mother is different from a foster mother.

Eight
Harper's Mom

There's no need to hide anymore. No need to slip into his father's car early and peek at Harper leaving his house for school and walking down the street, punching the air. No more finding reasons to go to a friend's house after school just to avoid him. Everything is out in the open now. Harper knows Calvin lives right next door. The funny thing is, Harper hasn't questioned Calvin about it. He hasn't asked Calvin why he didn't come over and welcome him to the neighborhood or ask to shoot hoops with him or skateboard or whatever. It's almost like Harper doesn't expect regular stuff to happen to him. It's kind of sad.

○ ● ○

On Monday Gavin and Richard and Calvin and Carlos
are walking down Ashby, heading to Mr. D.'s store
for candy. It's an early-dismissal day, and Calvin feels
free. Suddenly he hears a voice behind them.

All the boys turn around at the same time. They
turn back to Calvin once they realize that Harper
is calling *him*. He's already told his friends about
Harper's strange behavior at the movies.
They've all decided that, on top of everything
else, Harper is a little weird.

"You better find out
what he wants," Gavin
says.

The group walks on
to Mr. D.'s while Calvin
waits — reluctantly —
as Harper approaches.
There's a rare smile on
Harper's face, and Calvin
wonders why. He looks back at
his friends, but they've disap-
peared into the store. He's on his own.

"I'm going to see my mom. Do you want to go with me?"

"Uh," Calvin says.

"My foster mother doesn't know we got out of school early. She won't be expecting me until three."

Calvin remembers that his father won't be expecting him either. He has permission to go to Richard's and do homework. Then he and his friends planned to play basketball. "Okay," he says. He doesn't know if it's curiosity that he feels or just worry about what Harper might do if he turns him down.

Harper is silent as the two backtrack up Ashby and turn on Marin to where the street dead-ends at Miller's Park. Calvin wonders just how far they'll be going and what everyone will think when he doesn't catch up to them at Mr. D.'s.

But then, just as quickly, he wonders if Harper's mom lives in one of those homeless encampments under the freeway. Calvin doesn't want to go to a homeless encampment under the freeway.

Maybe Harper's mom is in some kind of shelter. Or perhaps they'll go into the park, where Harper's mother will be sitting on a bench with all her belongings in a shopping cart, wearing a big lawn-and-leaf bag as a shirt. Calvin saw a woman wearing a lawn-and-leaf bag as a shirt one time, and he couldn't help staring at her. He and his parents had been coming out of a restaurant, and she was standing there in the middle of the sidewalk, blocking their way with a cup in her hand. His father had reached in his pocket, pulled out two dollars, and dropped them in the cup.

She had smudges of dirt on her face, and her hair looked like it had never been combed. When she smiled, Calvin saw that she had two front teeth — on the top — missing. The teeth that were left were brown. "Thank you sooo much," she'd said, and Calvin had worried that she might hug him. And get bugs all over him.

When she was no longer in earshot, Calvin had said, "I don't like that woman."

"We don't know that woman, and we don't know what her life's been like," his father replied. "You be grateful that we have better circumstances."

His father's words had made him feel a little ashamed, and he'd thought about running back and giving her the change in his pocket. But he didn't.

● ● ●

Harper and Calvin don't go all the way into the park. They take a side street and Harper, still leading the way, walks through the open gate of the community garden. Calvin doesn't know what to think. What are they doing here? He knows about this place — though he's never been here — because his mother volunteers there on Wednesday mornings. She brings home vegetables all the time. She can get really excited over kale and cauliflower, but none of it excites Calvin the way french fries do.

He likes the look of the community garden. It's something surprising in the middle of the regular neighborhood street. He hears classical music coming out of a speaker attached to the toolshed at the back of the lot.

Then, from behind the shed comes a woman in overalls, wearing a red kerchief on her head and carrying a tray of seedlings. She stops in her tracks, puts the tray down, and comes to where he and Harper are standing. She hugs Harper and gives him a kiss on the cheek! Calvin is surprised.

Harper hugs the woman back, and that's when Calvin understands: The lady is Harper's mom.

Calvin looks from Harper to his mother and back to Harper again. He can see that she looks like the woman in the photograph on Harper's dresser but it's hard to put the two of them together as mother and son. She's small and pretty, and young-looking. Harper is big and likes to frown a lot.

"This is my friend Calvin, Mom," Harper says in a voice Calvin has never heard come out of him before. A nice voice. Not at all gruff.

Harper's mother turns to Calvin and extends her small hand. "I'm Aileen."

Calvin reaches out and shakes it.

"He's the one I went to the movies with. His dad is really nice," Harper says.

Harper noticed that Calvin's father is "really nice"? That's another big surprise.

"Um." Calvin pauses, because he doesn't know if he

can call Harper's mother by her first name. He's aware that lots of kids call adults by their first names, but his parents always insist he put a Mrs. or Ms. or Miss or Mr. before it. "Miss Aileen? What's that music for?"

"To make the plants grow better," Harper says.

Calvin frowns, feeling a little confused.

Harper's mother laughs. "Yes, supposedly classical music makes plants grow better."

Could that be true? Calvin wonders.

"That's what I'm doing my science-fair project on," Harper adds.

Calvin turns to stare at him. He didn't even think Harper would be doing a science-fair project. He figured he'd skip it, like he skips a lot of his work.

"Yeah," his mother says. "Harper's really excited about it. It's the sound waves traveling through the air to the plants, kind of stimulating them. He's using radishes — grown here and where he's staying."

Staying. Calvin thinks of that word. It sounds so temporary.

"I started the ones with no music at Mrs. Jeffers's old house," Harper says. "And I brought them with me."

Calvin is feeling a little uneasy. This is sounding

like a really interesting project, and it's sounding way more scientific than Calvin's. Harper can talk about sound waves and what sound waves do. Then he can come up with a really scientific-sounding hypothesis, and from that a prediction. Calvin wonders if Harper knows all that.

"You guys want some lemonade?" his mother asks cheerfully.

"Yeah," Harper says. They follow her to the tool-shed, where there's a miniature refrigerator. She reaches in and takes out two bottles of lemonade. She hands one to Calvin and one to Harper.

Calvin looks around. There's a cot in one corner with folded linens and a blanket on it. It looks like someone is using an upturned crate for a nightstand. There's a lamp on it and a CD player. At the foot of the cot is a box of folded clothes.

They go back outside, and Miss Aileen shows Calvin around the entire community garden.

"My mom volunteers here on Wednesdays," Calvin says.

"What's her name?"

"Valerie Vickers."

"Oh, Val," Miss Aileen says. "I know Val. Though I haven't seen her in a while."

"That's because she's in New Mexico taking care of my Grandma Kate. She broke her hip."

"Ouch!" Miss Aileen says, and Harper and Calvin laugh at the funny face she makes while saying the word.

Harper pulls a small package wrapped in Christmas paper out of his jeans pocket—though Christmas was months ago. He holds it out to his mother.

"What's this?" she asks.

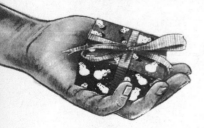

"A present," Harper tells her. "But don't open it now," he adds quickly. "Open it later." He looks at Calvin. Calvin wonders what it is.

● ● ●

As they leave, Calvin wants to ask all kinds of questions. Like, who's living in the toolshed? Because clearly, someone is living in there. He doesn't have to ask, though, because Harper explains things as soon as they get out onto the sidewalk.

"That's where my mom lives," he says flatly. "And it's where I lived too."

"In the toolshed?"

"Yeah. The people who own the land let her. We didn't have anywhere else to go. My mom lost her job, and then we didn't have the rent money."

Calvin is trying to take all this in. He can't imagine living in a toolshed.

"Someone found out and they called the child-protection people and then I had to be put in a foster home."

"Do you wish you lived with your mother?" Calvin asks.

"I *am* going to live with my mother. 'Cause she's going to get a job, and then we're going to get an apartment." Harper seems like he's sure about this.

"How often do you see her?"

"All the time. 'Cause I help her a lot in the garden because I love plants."

Calvin looks over at Harper, realizing that sometimes you just don't know what a person is all about, at all.

● ● ●

When they get to their houses, just before Calvin turns toward his front door, he says, "Harper . . ." The name still feels strange in his mouth.

"Huh?"

"Your mother is really, really nice."

Harper smiles one of his rare smiles. "I already know that," he says.

Nine

Turquoise Bracelet and
Necklace to Match

The next morning before school, on the play yard, Calvin tells Carlos and Gavin and Richard all about his experience the day before with Harper. He thinks they might find it funny: Harper's mother, living in a toolshed. But they just listen with mouths kind of hanging open. Finally Carlos says, "Wow. Harper lived in a toolshed."

"But it was pretty much fixed up and neat and it looked comfortable," Calvin explains.

"A toolshed," Richard repeats, squinting as if he's trying to imagine it.

Calvin glances around. He's relieved to see that no one's laughing. Everyone's looking kind of surprised

—and curious. He's glad. "Don't tell anyone, okay?" Calvin says.

"How come?" Richard asks.

"Because she was real nice, and how would you like it if you had that situation and someone started blabbing it all over school?"

Richard looks insulted. "I wasn't even going to say anything."

Calvin wonders if that is true.

● ● ●

When the bell rings and they file into the classroom, Calvin sees Ms. Shelby-Ortiz's morning journal topic on the whiteboard: "The Last Thing that Surprised You."

Calvin sits down and pulls out his journal. He turns to the next clean page and stares at it. He puts the date in the upper right corner. He stares some more. Then he begins:

This boy I know, his mom lives in a tool shed. I'm not going to say where because I don't want her to get in trouble. Because she has to live in the tool shed and he did too before he had to go to a foster house and have a foster mother who isn't really his mother but that's the only person to take care of him. He just said his father is somewhere. I saw this tool shed yesterday and it was cool. There was a cot like the kind you sleep in at camp and a box for her clothes and a radio/CD player and a small refrigerator just big enough for her food, I'm thinking. She's pretty and nice and I liked her so I'm going to pray that she gets a job and then she can get an apartment for herself and my friend.

Calvin looks at the words *my friend*. Is Harper his friend? He doesn't know. He has to admit, he's still a little afraid of him. But this morning, when they passed each other in the hall, Harper reached out and gave Calvin a soft punch on the arm. Later, when they passed each other again, Harper nodded at Calvin. Surprisingly, Calvin felt kind of . . . *proud*.

● ● ●

After school, Carlos and Gavin head off to soccer prac-
tice, and Richard says, "I want to go to the community
garden. I want to see Harper's mother."

Calvin's eyes get big. "Shhh," he says, looking
around. "What if Harper hears you?"

"He can't," Richard says. "This old lady picked him
up early. I saw her in the office when Ms. Shelby-Ortiz
sent me to get copy paper. Maybe he's got a dentist
appointment or something."

"Don't say anything, Richard. I wouldn't have told
you if I thought you were going to tell people."

"Okay, I won't. Can we go?"

"I guess."

● ● ●

When they walk through the garden gate, Calvin
doesn't see Harper's mom right away. Maybe she's in
the shed. There are two other women
there. One is down on her
knees, weeding, and the
other is watering some
plants toward the back
of the lot.

Calvin and Richard wander around and look at rows of plants. Richard walks ahead toward the toolshed.

"You can't go in there," Calvin says, regretting that he even told Richard and the others about Harper's mother.

"I just want to take a look."

The woman doing the weeding stands up, brushes her hands on her jeans. "Can I help you?" she asks.

"Um," says Calvin. "We're friends of Harper's, and me and Harper were here yesterday and I met his mother, and we just wanted to say hi."

"She borrowed my car to go get some mulch from the nursery. She should be back any minute."

"We can wait," Richard is quick to say.

The woman shrugs and goes back to her task.

"Come on," whispers Richard. "I just want to see what it looks like — inside."

Calvin hesitates. "We'll look inside for five seconds

and then we have to go." He doesn't have a good feeling about this.

Richard is already leading the way to the shed in the corner. Calvin looks around. He doesn't want to follow, but he doesn't really have a choice. At least the woman who was watering plants toward the back of the garden has moved closer to the street. The woman doing the weeding is on the far side of the garden as well.

Richard peeks in the window of the shed. Calvin waits behind him, not wanting to get too close. He looks around nervously again until Richard steps back. "That's cool. I could live in there," Richard says.

"Come on now. Let's get out of here."

"Hold on." Richard tries the door. It's not locked. "Let's go in."

"No, Richard. You wouldn't want anyone to just walk into your house when you weren't there."

"This isn't a house. It's a toolshed."

"You know what I mean."

But Richard opens the door and slips inside.

Calvin checks the street for Harper's mother.

It's a good thing he does, because just then he sees a blue minivan pull up in front of the garden. He watches until he sees Harper's mother jump out and go around to the back. She opens the hatch and stares at the contents of the cargo space. Finally she lifts a big plastic bag onto her shoulder. She holds it there with one hand, and with the other she slams the door shut.

Calvin slips around to the part of the shed hidden away from the street. He knocks on the window. He sees Richard's smiling face — he's pressing his nose against the windowpane from the inside, probably thinking he's some kind of comedian. Calvin mouths, *Come on,* and points toward the street.

Richard steps out of the shed and looks where Calvin's pointing. He closes the door behind him. They're making their way down the path between the spinach and peas, cucumbers and chard, when Miss Aileen notices them.

"Hey," she says, waving. She leans the bag of mulch against one of the raised beds full of soil and plants and comes over to them. "Where's Harper?" She has a big smile on her face.

Calvin and Richard look at each other.

"I think he went somewhere with Mrs. Jeffers," Calvin says.

Harper's mom keeps smiling, but it's not as big a smile as it was just seconds before. "What are you guys doing here?" she asks, but in a friendly way.

"I just wanted to show Richard the community garden," Calvin says, feeling a little guilty. Calvin knows that Richard was more curious about the shed than the actual garden.

Harper's mother nods.

"Well, I guess we'll go now," Calvin says.

Harper's mother nods again, then holds up her palm. "Wait. I have something for you." She reaches down and picks something green with curly-edged leaves.

"Kale. Fresh and organic," she says, handing bunches to Calvin *and* Richard. Richard looks at the leaves in his hand. "Thank you," he manages, though his smile looks forced.

"Thank you," Calvin says, and then he notices something. The bracelet on Harper's mom's arm looks just like a bracelet his mother has. The one with the matching necklace. It's silver with turquoise stones. It looks *exactly* like the bracelet his mother wears.

Suddenly Calvin realizes that it *is* his mother's bracelet. It all comes back in a rush: Harper having to use the bathroom, which happens to be right next to Calvin's parents' bedroom; the length of time Harper took in there; Harper giving his mother a gift wrapped in Christmas paper and telling her not to open it until later.

Calvin thinks about this all the way to Richard's. He thinks about it during their game of one-on-one basketball. He thinks about it as he walks home, as he does his homework, as he goes into his parents' room and looks in the jewelry box and sees only the turquoise necklace. He's still thinking about it at the kitchen table as he sits across from his father, eating his father's version of spaghetti and looking at boiled kale. Maybe he should have put the kale in the very back of the refrigerator. It's bad enough that his dad's spaghetti is just pasta and store-bought spaghetti sauce. It isn't very good.

"Dad," he says.

"Hmm?"

"I think Harper took Mom's turquoise bracelet."

His father looks up from his dinner. "That's quite an accusation. Do you have a good reason for thinking so?"

"I saw Mom's bracelet on Harper's mother's arm. Today."

"Where'd you see his mother?"

"At the community garden, after school. On the way to Richard's," he adds quickly, because he only had permission to go to Richard's to do homework. He'd already told his dad yesterday all about Harper's mom living in a shed at the community garden. His father had lectured him again about how one never knows what another person is going through.

His dad raises an eyebrow. "Just because she has the same bracelet your mom has doesn't mean Harper stole it. You can't think that Harper stole it just on a hunch."

"But I looked in Mom's jewelry box, and the matching necklace was there but not the bracelet."

"Maybe she took the bracelet with her."

"But she always wears them together. Can you call her?"

"I'm not going to disturb your mother about this when she's probably tired and stressed-out from taking care of your grandmother. We'll find out when she gets home."

"But—"

"You shouldn't accuse someone of stealing unless you have proof. That's no proof, Calvin. Subject closed."

It *is* proof — to Calvin. He hates when his father bends over backwards to be Mr. Fair. In his gut Calvin knows that the bracelet on Miss Aileen's arm is his own mother's. But he has to wait for proof, just to be *fair*. Calvin scrunches up his mouth at the thought of it.

Okay. He'll wait. And when his mother gets back and complains about her missing bracelet — when she tells his father that she always keeps it in her jewelry box when she isn't wearing it — then he'll have his proof.

Ten
Science Fair

The march of the science projects: That's what it looks like on the yard and in the hall leading to the gymnasium Thursday morning before school. Ms. Shelby-Ortiz told them that the class could start bringing in their projects the day before the fair, and Calvin almost decided to wait. His plan was to just check out the parade of display boards and science paraphernalia and then, on the day of the actual science fair, he'd *unmask* his own.

But he changed his mind. He decided he might as well bring his project in a day early too. That way, while he was setting up his display, he could get an even closer look at his competition. Now as he glances around the gym to see if his project really is the most original, he's happy to decide that yes — his is, absolutely, the most original and the most interesting.

There go the blue carnations, he thinks, catching sight one of the second-graders with a vase of blue carnations in blue water. And there go not one but *two* clay volcanoes being carried on plywood boards. Wait until Richard gets a load of that.

Carlos, with his big white display board that's nearly empty, has begun to set up behind him. Calvin looks over his shoulder. The board has a few index cards posted on it and some kind of graph. He watches Carlos pull two small jars with holes in the lids out of a small box. He dumps the contents of one jar into a little glass dish and the contents of the other into another glass dish, probably to see what his whole setup will look like. He stands back and checks it, then returns both dishes' contents to the jars.

Curious, Calvin moves over to Carlos's table and is immediately grossed out. The jars are full of wiggly brown mealworms and fat, cream-colored wax worms. "Ugh, what are those for?"

"Remember, my project is about seeing which

worms my geckos prefer — wax worms or meal-worms. I want people to see the real live food."

"Couldn't you just draw a picture?"

"I can't draw that good. Anyway, I want people to be grossed out. The judges will probably give me a better score that way."

Carlos has a point, Calvin thinks. He frowns at the writhing worms. He looks up at Carlos hurriedly writing *Wax Worms* and *Mealworms* on index cards and placing the cards next to the empty dishes.

Okay. So he's got a bit more competition than he'd thought.

He wanders over to Richard and his volcano. Someone — he's sure it wasn't Richard — has painted an island scene on Richard's display board and made palm trees with twisted brown wrapping paper and yarn. That 3D effect might catch a lot of the judges' attention. It's kind of creative, and adults love creativity. He realizes he's losing some of his confidence.

Then in comes Harper with his mom. Calvin is surprised to see Harper's mom at school. She's carrying the display board, and Harper is carrying two trays of radishes.

Even from Calvin's position, he can see a huge difference in the trays of radishes. A huge difference. And everybody's looking at Harper's pretty mom. The other kids are all fascinated by her.

On Harper's display board, red construction-paper letters form the questions *With or Without Music? (Do Sound Waves Nourish Plants?)*. Immediately Calvin has a sinking feeling. A bunch of people will want to know the answer to that, he's sure. He looks around. He bets more people have plants than have, say, *geckos*. Plenty of folks have gardens, and they're going to want to know the answer to that question. Harper might get lots of points.

Who's going to care if boys can see an optical illusion

faster than girls? Calvin wonders. And they can't. At least not the boys he chose. Maybe Ralph or Carlos's cousin Bernardo would have done better. But it's too late.

Harper's mom is setting up a question card in the middle of the display board. *Guess!* it says. *Then lift the card to see the answer.* So his project is interactive. That's sure to get him even more points.

Calvin shakes his head and continues to fool with his own display. He angles the data sheets on his table, then repositions the sample tests on his board. Next he busies himself centering the letters of his title across the top of the middle panel of his display: *Whose Brain Is Faster? Boys' or Girls'?* Was that a good question? He wonders.

Finally the bell rings. Time to go to class.

● ● ●

"Calvin, let's go," his father calls up the stairs the next afternoon, when it's time for them to leave for the science fair. Calvin had arranged with his father to go home after school so he could change into fresh clothes. He figured a crisply-ironed shirt and pants might impress the judges, somehow. And it was a good thing he did. He was there when his mother called to wish him luck.

"When are you coming home?" he'd asked her for the zillionth time.

"Won't be long now," she'd told him. "Be patient."

Now Calvin is tying his shoelaces and feeling sorry for himself. He's been counting on getting the new Wuju Legend video game. He's imagined playing it and other people wanting to play with it, and him deciding who gets to play with it. But now he doesn't think it's going to happen.

In the car his dad looks over at him and says, "I'm going to drop you off, then run to take care of something at work. I'll only be gone thirty minutes, tops. Are you okay with that?"

Calvin nods. "Yeah. That's fine."

● ● ●

The gymnasium is packed with parents, kids, and teachers — and there's a long table against one wall with paper cups of punch and plates of cookies and chips. Mrs. Broadie, the cafeteria lady, stands guard over it, making sure kids take one cup and one plate and that they don't go through the line again.

Antonia's display is the biggest in the auditorium. He'd noticed it yesterday. It's as tall as she is. How did she find a display board that tall? She needs it. The panels are packed with stuff. There's a topic in big blue letters (*Which Brand Pops the Best?*), papers and graphs (what are the graphs for?), and five different brands of popcorn stuck to the board — using two-sided tape, probably. On the table in front of the display board are five small bowls of popcorn.

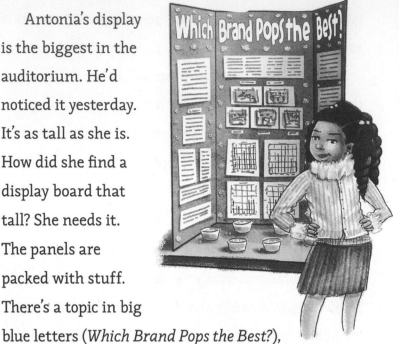

It seems to Calvin to be a lot of blah, blah, blah showing nothing. Fancy and spectacular nothing. Yeah — like where's the hypothesis? Where's the prediction? He sees the panel of parents with their pens and clipboards, appearing dazzled by the display. He wants to rush over to them and point out that there is no real hypothesis. And the pictures of Antonia and her friends tasting each brand and ranking them and then counting the unpopped kernels and posting them beside each brand — what's all that but filler? He thinks, *She's obviously trying to fill up her display board. She must feel she can get more points on just the size of her board and all the stuff on it...*

He wishes his dad would hurry up and get there. He paces a bit, stops, checks his own display board again, and is dismayed to still see a lot of blank space.

Just then the parent judges turn and head his way with their clipboards at the ready. His throat feels like it's closing. There will be questions. Is he ready?

"Ahhh," one of the fathers says, looking at the question below the title at the top of Calvin's display: *Do Boys See Optical Illusions Faster than Girls?* It's Antonia's dad. Calvin has seen him dropping off Antonia in front of the school. Calvin also recognizes Gregory Johnson's mother in the group. He met her at Gregory's skateboard party. Now she squints at his hypothesis and marks the paper on her clipboard. She smiles at him. "Interesting question," she says. "And prediction," she adds, looking at the sentences he'd written in big, red letters: *Boys are faster at every-thing. So, yes.* She peers at Calvin's posted samples of optical illusions. Then she checks his conclusion. She smiles at him again.

He's ready for questions.

"Good job," she says. "You might have wanted your results to be different, but I'm glad to see that you posted them as they were. Very good," she says again, and then writes something else on her paper.

That's a good sign, Calvin thinks. He looks at the rest of the small group as they jot down notes and score stuff. Then they move on. He watches after them, unable to judge his chances by their expressions. It looks like they're trying to keep their faces as blank as possible.

Calvin's dad finally arrives. He can see him making his way over but stopping here and there to check out the other projects. He's standing near Gavin, who's demonstrating a method of separating salt from pepper with the use of a comb he runs through his hair over and over to build up static. Parents and the panel seem fascinated by this, like it's some kind of circus trick. Gavin looks thrilled to be receiving so much attention.

At one point he glances over at Calvin and pumps his arm with confidence. Calvin smiles weakly and feels his optimism slip even more.

As if that weren't enough, he notices a cluster of other parents around Harper's display. *And* Harper is wearing a *tie*. Oh, no! The judges are probably loving that. That's just how parents think. He should have put on a tie, too.

Harper's mother, standing proudly nearby, has even thought to provide background classical music on the CD player he'd seen in the shed.

That's what's drawing the parents, Calvin thinks. *That's what's drawing them like flies to honey.* He checks their expressions. They're looking all *dreamy-eyed.* They're gazing at the radishes like they're diamonds or something. He doesn't stand a chance with parents acting like that — and probably influencing the judges. He feels like sitting down, but he knows he has to just stand there with a ready smile on his face waiting for someone to come by and show an interest in his project. It's a little bit miserable.

● ● ●

At last Calvin's father gets to his table. He seems to be about to give Calvin some words of encouragement when Mr. Brown, the principal, climbs the stairs to the stage with a few papers in his hand. He clears his throat. He taps the microphone and asks the stupid question "Can everybody hear me?" All eyes turn to him. *Too late now,* Calvin thinks. *Here it comes. Here comes failure.*

And here comes the long, boring talk about the importance of scientific inquiry and igniting curiosity in a child's mind and creating environments that nourish the desire for investigation and on and on and blah, blah, blah.

Calvin has to listen to all of this before Mr. Brown gets to the announcement of the first-, second-, and third-place winners. And wouldn't you know, he's starting with the third-place winner. Calvin has never even thought about third place.

But then it occurs to him: He could actually get third place. What a letdown that would be. To be *third* best.

He turns his attention back to Mr. Brown just as he's calling Antonia up to the stage to receive her third-place white ribbon and some kind of certificate. He can't believe all that empty glitz is being rewarded.

Just as Calvin is wondering what his father might give him for winning second place, Mr. Brown calls up Richard's brother, Darnell Woolsy. Darnell Woolsy? What did he do again? Calvin didn't pay any attention to Darnell Woolsy and his project. He searches the room to see Darnell leaving his table to mount the steps to the stage. The topic on his display board says: *Is Yawning Contagious?*

Really? Everyone already knows the answer to that. It's *yes*. How did Darnell get a problem, a hypothesis, a procedure, results, and a conclusion out of something that everyone already knows the answer to? This contest must be rigged. He looks down at Darnell's table.

Sure enough, his board is packed with graphs and pictures of his brothers and his mother and father yawning. Oh, the *unfairness* of it! Calvin watches him climb the stairs to the stage to receive his red ribbon and shake Mr. Brown's hand.

After a few words congratulating Darnell, Mr. Brown takes the mike off the stand and begins to walk back and forth as he speaks. He talks about how pleasantly surprised he was by the winner of the first-place ribbon. How he's seen this really wonderful side of this person who won first prize, and how he hopes this is just the beginning of more good stuff to come. And that's when Calvin knows it's going to be Harper. Mr. Brown can't be looking for more good stuff to come from Calvin.

Calvin glances over at Harper. He's fiddling with his display board, looking completely unaware that he's the person Mr. Brown is talking about. In fact, he doesn't seem like he's even listening.

So when Mr. Brown calls Harper's name, he looks up, puzzled. His mother turns to him and gives him a big hug. Harper appears even more bewildered. She says something to him and leads him to the bottom of the stage stairs.

Harper still looks confused as he climbs them — and when Mr. Brown congratulates him and puts the blue ribbon in his hand, he stands there looking speechless. "Thank you," he mumbles. He goes back down the stairs and receives handshakes and hugs from the panel of parents.

Calvin realizes then that his lip is curling slightly. He glances up at his father and sees him actually smiling. He looks down at Calvin and says, "If it can't be you, then I'm glad it's Harper."

Calvin nods slowly. He guesses he feels the same.

His father looks down at him again. "Come on," his dad says.

"Huh?"

"Let's go congratulate Harper."

Eleven
Saturday

Calvin's lying in bed, staring at the ceiling and rehashing all the events of the day before. Why does life have to have disappointments? Why can't things always go as planned? Why is it that something that you don't see coming . . . well, comes? He thinks about how his mother had called just before they were leaving for the science fair to wish him luck. Now even she's going to be disappointed.

Or maybe not. His father didn't act disappointed. He just said things like, "You win some, you lose some," as they were driving home. Yeah, yeah. But is that the point? To Calvin the point is that he's not getting the latest Wuju Legend video game. That's the

real point. He sighs. He might as well get up and pre-
pare for a boring Saturday.

But the doorbell rings just as Calvin is dragging
himself down the stairs to see what's for breakfast.
He peeks through the peephole and
there's Harper's big face peek-
ing back at him. Calvin opens
the door to Harper standing on
his porch with the blue ribbon
pinned to his shirt.

"Why are you wearing that?"
Calvin asks before he can stop himself. He braces for an angry response.
Harper could think Calvin is making fun of him. But there's no angry
response.

"Because I want to," Harper
says simply.

"You want to come in?" Calvin asks.

Harper shrugs but steps inside. He has something, Calvin notices. Something small and hidden in
his closed hand.

Calvin leads the way to the kitchen. His dad is standing at the counter, stirring pancake batter. "Hey, Harper," he says. "How's it going?"

"Fine," Harper says. "Your dad cooks?" he whispers to Calvin.

Calvin sits down at the table. "Yeah. Sometimes," he answers.

Just then the doorbell rings.

"Oh, shoot," Calvin's dad says. "That must be Miss Viola from across the street. Her cat is missing, and I promised to post some fliers at Big Barn. Hope you guys can wait for your pancakes. She's a talker."

They both shrug at the same time, and Calvin feels a strange sense of . . . *companionship* with Harper. Just for a moment.

"Here," Harper says as he glances at Calvin's dad's retreating back. He pushes something toward Calvin.

"What's this?" The small item is wrapped in brown paper and taped closed.

Calvin unwraps it. It's his mother's bracelet! His mouth drops open. He's speechless.

"My mom told me I should

give it back. 'Cause I told her I took it." Harper looks down at his hands.

"You told your mom that?" Calvin is surprised.

"Yeah."

"Did she get mad at you?"

"No."

Calvin looks at the bracelet. "Thanks," he says. He slips it into his shirt pocket. Funny: He imagined being proven right would feel good. It doesn't feel all that great. He'll just return it to his mother's jewelry box and maybe not even mention it to his dad. Just yet . . .

● ● ●

The pancakes aren't that bad. They're not as good as his mother's pancakes, but still. He watches Harper drown his in butter and syrup and then cut a huge forkful to stuff into his mouth.

Calvin's father, who's only eating oatmeal for breakfast these days, is now loading the dishwasher with last night's dinner dishes. "So, Harper," he says, "how does it feel to be a first-place winner?"

"Good," Harper answers, before cramming his mouth with another giant forkful. He chews, swallows, then says, "I'm gonna get the new Wuju Legend video game. My mother's been saving and saving. She sells crochet stuff she makes at the swap meet. She promised me she'd get it even if I didn't win if I just tried to do a good job."

Calvin looks at his father quickly to see if those remarks have had an impact. But his father just smiles at Harper and nods.

"Hey," Harper says. "When we finish, you wanna go out and shoot some hoops?"

This is weird. Calvin was thinking that even before Harper — *Monster Boy?* — asked the question. Two

weeks ago, he would have never imagined Harper sitting at his kitchen table, eating pancakes, and then asking him if he wanted to go outside and shoot hoops. Funny how life can be.

Now he notices that Harper has a hopeful expression on his face. And that his hopeful appearance is fading a tiny bit. He's already starting to look like he's thinking Calvin is probably going to turn him down. But Calvin *doesn't* turn him down. He doesn't even consider it.

"Yeah, sure," he says, and then realizes that it's going to be kind of fun living next door to Harper. He'll always have someone to shoot hoops with, and maybe — just maybe — from time to time Harper will let him borrow that latest Wuju Legend video game. Until Calvin gets his own, that is.

Karen English is a Gryphon Award winner, a Coretta Scott King Honor recipient, and the author of the Nikki and Deja series. Her chapter books have been praised for their accessible writing, authentic characters, and satisfying story lines. She is a former elementary school teacher and lives in Los Angeles, California.

Laura Freeman has illustrated several books for children, including ten chapter books about the kids of Carver Elementary. She grew up in New York City and now lives near Atlanta, Georgia, with her husband and two sons. Her drawings for this book were inspired by her children, as well as her own childhood.

Read more about the kids of Carver Elementary in these other great books:

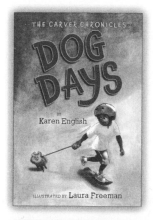